S0-ABC-817

Copyright © 2003 by Running Press
Illustrations © 2003 by Greg Hildebrandt
For information regarding print editions or original
Hildebrandt art, please contact Spiderwebart Gallery,
973 770 8189 or go to http://www.spiderwebart.com.

All rights reserved under the Pan-American and
International Copyright Conventions.

Printed in China

*This book may not be reproduced in whole or in part, in any form or
by any means, electronic or mechanical, including photocopying, recording, or
by any information storage and retrieval system now known or
hereafter invented, without written permission from the publisher.*

9   8   7   6   5   4   3   2   1
Digit on the right indicates the number of this printing

Library of Congress Control Number: 2002115137

ISBN 978-0-7624-3221-9

Illustrated by Greg Hildebrandt
Designed by Frances J. Soo Ping Chow
Typography: Centaur
Text adapted and abridged by Elizabeth Haserick

This book may be ordered by mail from the publisher.
*But try your bookstore first!*

Published by Courage Books, an imprint of
Running Press Book Publishers
2300 Chestnut Street
Philadelphia, PA 19103-4371

Visit us on the web!
www.runningpress.com

# The Wonderful Wizard of
# OZ

Dorothy lived on the great Kansas prairies, with her Uncle Henry and Aunt Em. Their house was only one room. There was no attic and the only cellar was a small hole in the ground called a cyclone cellar, where the family could go in case a great whirlwind arose.

Gray prairie surrounded the gray house. Aunt Em and Uncle Henry were gray as well. It was Toto, a little black dog with long silky hair, who saved Dorothy from growing as gray as her other surroundings. Dorothy played with him and loved him dearly.

Today they were not playing. Uncle Henry looked anxiously at the sky, which was more gray than usual. Dorothy was looking at the sky too. Aunt Em was washing dishes. A cyclone was coming. Uncle Henry went to the sheds to look after the cows and horses.

Aunt Em dropped her work and came to the door. One glance told her the cyclone was close. "Quick Dorothy!" she screamed. "Run for the cellar!"

Toto ran under the bed, and Dorothy tried to get him. Aunt Em, badly frightened, threw open the trap door in the floor and climbed down into the cellar. Dorothy caught Toto at last and started to follow her aunt. When she was halfway across the room there came a great shriek of wind, and the house shook so hard that she fell to the floor.

Then a strange thing happened. The house whirled around two or three times and rose slowly through the air, until it was caught up and carried by the cyclone for many miles.

It was very dark, and the wind howled horribly around her, but Dorothy found she was riding quite easily.

Toto ran about the room, barking loudly; but Dorothy sat quite still on the floor and waited to see what would happen. Finally she crawled to her bed and fell asleep.

Dorothy was awakened suddenly and sat up. The house was not moving. Bright sunshine came in the window, and she ran to the door to look outside.

The country outside was beautiful, with patches of bright green grass, trees bearing rich and luscious fruits, and gorgeous flowers. Unusual and beautiful birds flew by, while a small brook sparkled.

Dorothy noticed an odd group of people coming toward her. They seemed about as tall as her, but they looked many years older. Three were men and one a woman, all oddly dressed. They wore round hats that rose to a small point a foot above their heads, with little bells around the brims that tinkled. The men wore all blue, while the woman wore a white gown that glistened like diamonds. The men, Dorothy thought, were about as old as Uncle Henry, for two of them had beards. But the little woman was much older.

Seeing Dorothy, they paused and whispered amongst themselves,

as if afraid to come farther. But the little old woman walked up to Dorothy, made a low bow and said in a sweet voice:

"You are welcome, most noble Sorceress, to the land of the Munchkins. They are so grateful to you for having killed the Wicked Witch of the East, and for setting their people free from slavery to her."

The old woman pointed to the corner of Dorothy's house. Dorothy looked, and gave a little cry of fright. There, indeed, were two feet sticking out from under the house, shod in silver shoes with pointed toes.

"I am the Munchkins' friend, the Good Witch of the North. There is another Good Witch, in the South. Those who dwelt in the East and the West were, indeed, wicked witches. Now that you have killed one of them, there is but one Wicked Witch in all the Land of Oz—the one who lives in the West."

Just then the Munchkins, who had been standing silently by, gave a loud shout and pointed to the corner of the house where the Wicked Witch had been lying. The feet of the dead Witch had disappeared entirely, and nothing was left but the silver shoes.

The Wicked Witch of the East had dried up in the sun, but the silver shoes were still left.

The Good Witch handed them to Dorothy to keep.

"The Witch of the East was proud of those Silver Shoes," said one of the Munchkins, "and there is some charm connected with them; but what it is we never knew."

Dorothy asked the Munchkins if they could help her find her way back to Kansas.

The Munchkins and the Witch shook their heads.

"You must go to the Emerald City. Perhaps the Great Wizard Oz will help you," said the Good Witch of the North.

"Where is this city?" asked Dorothy.

"It is exactly in the center of the country, and is ruled by Oz, the Great Wizard."

"Is he a good man?" inquired the girl anxiously.

"He is a good Wizard. Whether he is a man or not I cannot tell, for I have never seen him."

"How can I get there?" asked Dorothy.

"You must walk. It is a long journey, through a country that is sometimes pleasant and sometimes dangerous. However, I will use all the magic I know of to keep you from harm. I will give you my kiss as protection, and no one will dare injure you," said the Good Witch of the North.

She came close to Dorothy and kissed her gently on the forehead. Then she pointed to the road to the Emerald City, which was paved with yellow bricks, said goodbye, and disappeared. The Munchkins wished Dorothy well, and departed through the trees.

Dorothy put on her blue and white checked gingham dress and pink sunbonnet, filled a little basket with bread, and put on the Silver Shoes that had belonged to the Witch of the East.

She started down the road paved with yellow bricks. Around her were neat fences painted a dainty blue, fields of grain and vegetables in abundance, and once in a while a house that was round with a big dome

roof. All the houses were painted blue, for in this country of the East, blue was the favorite color.

The people came out to look at her and bow low as she went by; for everyone knew she had destroyed the Wicked Witch of the East and set them free from bondage.

Toward evening, Dorothy came to a large Munchkin house, where men and women were dancing and singing to celebrate their freedom from the bondage of the Wicked Witch.

Dorothy ate a hearty supper and was waited upon by the rich Munchkin, Boq. She sat and watched the people dance, then slept soundly in the house until morning.

Dorothy bade her friends good-bye and started again down the yellow brick road. When she had gone several miles she stopped to rest, sitting on a fence beside the road. Not far away a Scarecrow in an old blue Munchkin suit was placed high on a pole in the middle of a field, to keep birds away from the ripe corn.

Dorothy gazed at the Scarecrow. Suddenly, the Scarecrow slowly winked at her. She thought she must have been mistaken at first, for none of the scarecrows in Kansas ever wink; but presently the figure nodded its head to her in a friendly way. She went up to the Scarecrow.

"Good day," said the Scarecrow.

"Did you speak?" asked the girl, in wonder.

"Certainly," answered the Scarecrow. "How do you do?"

"I'm pretty well, thank you," replied Dorothy politely. "How do you do?"

"I'm not feeling well," said the Scarecrow, with a smile, "for it is very tedious being perched up here night and day to scare away crows. If you will please take away the pole which is stuck up my back I shall be greatly obliged to you."

Dorothy lifted the figure off the pole for, being stuffed with straw, it was quite light.

"Thank you very much," said the Scarecrow. "Who are you? And where are you going?"

"My name is Dorothy," said the girl, "and I am going to the Emerald City, to ask the Great Oz to send me back home."

"Do you think," the Scarecrow asked, "that Oz would give me some brains?" For he was stuffed, and had no brains.

"If you will come with me, I'll ask Oz to do all he can for you," Dorothy replied.

"Thank you," he answered gratefully.

They walked back to the road. After a while they came to a dark forest. Suddenly there was a deep groan nearby. A man, made entirely of tin, was standing beside a tree that was partially chopped through, an uplifted axe in his hands.

"Did you groan?" asked Dorothy.

"Yes," answered the tin man, "I did. I've been groaning for more than a year, and no one has ever heard me before or come to help me. Please get an oil can from my cottage and oil my joints. They are rusted so badly that I cannot move them at all; if I am well-oiled I shall soon be all right again."

Dorothy ran into the cottage and found the oil can, then she returned and oiled all of the man's joints.

The Tin Woodman gave a sigh of satisfaction and lowered his axe.

"This is a great comfort," he said. "I have been holding that axe in the air ever since I rusted, and I'm glad to be able to put it down at last. I might have stood there always if you had not come along," he said; "so you have certainly saved my life. How did you happen to be here?"

"We are on our way to the Emerald City to see the Great Oz," she answered.

"Why do you wish to see Oz?" he asked.

"I want him to send me back to Kansas, and the Scarecrow wants him to put a few brains into his head," she replied.

The Tin Woodman appeared to think deeply for a moment. Then he said:

"Do you suppose Oz could give me a heart?"

"Why, I guess so," Dorothy answered. "It would be as easy as to give the Scarecrow brains."

"True," the Tin Woodman returned. "So, if you will allow me to join your party, I will also go to the Emerald City and ask Oz to help me."

"Come along," said the Scarecrow heartily, and Dorothy added that she would be pleased to have his company.

The Tin Woodman had asked Dorothy to put the oil can in her basket. "For," he said, "if I should get caught in the rain and rust again, I would need the oil can badly."

The travelers continued on the yellow brick road. Suddenly, from the woods there came a terrible roar, and the next moment a great Lion bounded into the road. With one blow of his paw he sent the Scarecrow spinning over and over to the edge of the road, and then he struck at the Tin Woodman with his sharp claws. But, to the Lion's surprise, he could make no impression on the tin, although the Woodman fell over in the road and lay still.

Little Toto, now that he had an enemy to face, ran barking toward the Lion, and the great beast had opened his mouth to bite the dog, when Dorothy rushed forward and slapped the Lion upon his nose as hard as she could, while she cried out:

"Don't you dare bite Toto!"

"I didn't bite him," said the Lion, rubbing his nose where Dorothy had hit him.

"No, but you tried to," she retorted. "You are nothing but a big coward."

"I know it," said the Lion, hanging his head in shame. "I've always known it. But how can I help it?"

"Come with us to see Oz, and he will give you courage," said Dorothy.

"Then, if you don't mind, I'll go with you," said the Lion, "for my life is simply unbearable without a bit of courage."

"You will be very welcome," answered Dorothy, "for you will help to keep away the other wild beasts."

So once more the little company set off upon their journey.

After a while the forest grew very thick, dark, and gloomy. Strange noises came from the depths of the forest.

The travelers came upon a deep gulf across the road. The Tin Woodman chopped down a large tree, so that they could cross the gulf. They had just started to cross the tree-bridge when a sharp growl made them all look up, and to their horror they saw running toward them two great beasts with bodies like bears and heads like tigers.

"They are the Kalidahs!" said the Cowardly Lion, beginning to tremble.

Dorothy grabbed Toto and crossed the bridge. The Scarecrow and the Tin Woodman followed. The Lion crossed the bridge, then turned to roar at the Kalidahs, who paused, but seeing they were bigger than him, and remembering that there were two of them and only one of the Lion, the Kalidahs again rushed forward.

The Tin Woodman began to chop the tree at once, and, just as the two Kalidahs were nearly across, the tree fell with a crash into the gulf, carrying the ugly, snarling brutes with it, and both were dashed to pieces on the sharp rocks at the bottom.

This adventure made the travelers more anxious than ever to get out of the forest. They walked quickly, and finally came upon a swiftly flowing river. The Tin Woodman took his axe and began to chop down small trees to make a raft. When the raft was finished, the four travelers got on. They got along quite well at first, but when they reached the middle of the river the swift current swept the raft downstream, farther and farther away from the road of yellow brick. The water grew so deep that the long poles the Tin Woodman and the Scarecrow were using to push the raft could not touch the bottom.

"This is bad," said the Tin Woodman, "for if we cannot get to land, we shall be carried into the country of the Wicked Witch of the West, and she will enchant us and make us her slaves."

"We must certainly get to the Emerald City if we can," the Scarecrow said, and he pushed so hard on his long pole that it stuck fast in the mud at the bottom of the river. Then, before he could pull it out again or let go, the raft was swept away, and the poor Scarecrow was left clinging to the pole in the middle of the river.

The Lion sprang into the water, and the Tin Woodman caught hold of his tail. Then the Lion swam toward the shore. Upon reaching the shore, the travelers made their way back to the Scarecrow, still stuck in the middle of the river.

Just then a Stork flew by, who saved the Scarecrow from the river. The Scarecrow was much obliged.

When the Scarecrow found himself among his friends again, he was so happy that he hugged them all. "Thank you," Dorothy told the Stork, and then the kind Stork flew into the air and was soon out of sight.

The travelers walked along until they came to a large field of scarlet poppies, whose odor makes anyone who breathes it fall asleep. If the sleeper is not carried away from the scent of the flowers, he sleeps on and on forever. Presently Dorothy fell asleep.

"What shall we do?" asked the Tin Woodman.

"If we leave her here she will die," said the Lion. "The smell of the flowers is killing us all. I myself can scarcely keep my eyes open. I will run fast, and try to reach the edge of the field."

Toto and Dorothy were asleep, but the Scarecrow and Tin Woodman, not being made of flesh, were not troubled by the scent of the flowers. The Scarecrow and Tin Woodman picked up Toto and put the dog in Dorothy's lap and carried her. It seemed that the great carpet of deadly flowers would never end. At last, they came upon the Lion, fast asleep among the poppies only a short distance from the end of the poppy bed. Beyond it lay green grassy fields.

"We can do nothing for him," said the Tin Woodman, sadly; "for he is much too heavy to lift. We must leave him here to sleep on forever, and perhaps he will dream that he has found courage at last."

They carried Dorothy and Toto farther, and laid them gently on the ground, far away from the deadly smell of the poppies. Suddenly, the woodman heard a low growl, and saw a great yellow wildcat chasing a little gray field mouse. The cat's mouth was wide open, showing two rows of sharp teeth. Its eyes were red. Even though he had no heart the Woodman knew it was wrong to kill such a pretty, helpless creature. Raising his axe, he chopped the wildcat's head off.

The field mouse, now that it was safe from its enemy, drew near and said, in a squeaky little voice:

"Oh thank you, ever so much, for saving my life. I am the Queen of the Field Mice. Let my subjects repay your brave deed by granting you a wish."

The Tin Woodman and the Scarecrow wished for the mice to save their friend the Cowardly Lion. The Queen sent for all her subjects to come with a piece of string, to pull the Cowardly Lion out of the poppy field on a cart that the Tin Woodman made out of tree branches.

The mice were harnessed to the cart, and with the Woodman and the Scarecrow pushing from behind, soon the Lion was out of the poppy field. Dorothy awoke and thanked the little mice warmly for saving her companion from death.

Then the mice were unharnessed from the cart and scampered away through the grass to their homes. The Queen of the Mice was the last to leave.

"If ever you need us again," she said, "come out into the field and call, and we shall hear you and come to your assistance. Good-bye!"

"Good-bye!" they all answered, and away the Queen ran.

After this they sat down beside the Lion until he should awaken.

The Cowardly Lion awoke after awhile, and was very glad to find himself still alive.

When the Lion was feeling quite himself again, they all started down the yellow brick road. The country was beautiful. The fences and houses beside the road were painted green. The people dressed in a lovely emerald-green color and wore peaked hats like those of the Munchkins.

"This must be the Land of Oz," said Dorothy, "and we are surely getting near the Emerald City."

Soon there was a beautiful green glow in the sky just before them.

As they walked on, the green glow became brighter. By afternoon they came to the great wall that surrounded the City. It was high and thick and of a bright green color.

In front of them was a big gate, studded with emeralds that glittered in the sun. There was a bell beside the gate, which Dorothy rang. The big gate swung slowly open, and they all walked into a high arched room, its walls glistening with emeralds.

Before them stood a little man about the size of the Munchkins. He wore all green, and even his skin was of a greenish tint. At his side was a large green box.

The man asked, "What do you wish in the Emerald City?"

"We came here to see the Great Oz," said Dorothy.

The man was very surprised at this answer. "Few have seen Oz," he said. But I am the Guardian of the Gates, and I will take you to his palace. First you must put on these green glasses so that the brightness and glory of the Emerald City won't blind you. Even those who live in the city must wear spectacles night and day."

He opened the big box. It was filled with spectacles of every size and shape. The Guardian of the Gates found a pair that fit each of the travelers, and put the spectacles over their eyes.

Then the Guardian of the Gates put on his own glasses and told them he was ready to show them to the palace. Taking a big golden key from a peg on the wall, he opened another gate, and they all followed him into the streets of the Emerald City.

Even with their eyes protected by the green spectacles, Dorothy and her friends were at first dazzled by the brilliance of the wonderful city. The streets were lined with houses built of green marble and sparkling emeralds. The pavement was the same green marble, and where the blocks joined together, rows of emeralds glittered in the sun. The window panes were of green glass; even the sky above the city had a green tint, and the rays of the sun were green.

There were many people walking about, all dressed in green clothes, and with greenish skin. They looked at Dorothy and her strangely assorted company with wondering eyes, and the children all ran away and hid behind their mothers when they saw the Lion; but no one spoke to them. Many shops stood in the street, and Dorothy saw that everything in them was green.

There seemed to be no horses, nor animals of any kind; the men carried things around in little green carts, which they pushed before them. Everyone seemed happy and contented and prosperous.

The travelers came to the palace in the middle of the city. There was a soldier before the door, dressed in a green uniform and with a long green beard.

"Here are strangers," the Guardian of the Gates said to him, "and they demand to see the Great Oz."

"Step inside," answered the soldier, "and I will carry your message to him."

They passed through the palace gates and were led into a lovely green room.

The soldier left to relay his message. They had to wait a long time before the soldier returned. At last, he came back, and said: "Oz will see you, but each one of you must enter his presence alone, and he will admit but one each day. Therefore, I will have you shown to rooms in the palace where you may rest in comfort."

The next morning a green maiden came to fetch Dorothy, and she dressed Dorothy in one of the prettiest gowns, made of green brocaded satin. Dorothy put on a green silk apron and tied a green ribbon around Toto's neck, and they started for the throne room of the Great Oz.

Dorothy entered the throne room. It was a big, round room with a high arched roof, and everything was covered with large emeralds. In the center of the roof was a great light which made the emeralds sparkle.

A big throne of green marble, shaped like a chair and sparkling with gems, stood in the middle of the room. In the center of the chair was an enormous bald head, without a body to support it.

As Dorothy gazed upon the head in wonder and fear, the eyes turned slowly and looked at her sharply and steadily. Then the mouth moved, and Dorothy heard a voice say:

"I am Oz, the Great and Terrible. Who are you, and why do you seek me?"

Dorothy took courage and answered:

"I am Dorothy, the Small and Meek. I have come to you for help."

The eyes looked at her thoughtfully for a full minute. Then the voice asked:

"Where did you get the Silver Shoes?"

"I got them from the Wicked Witch of the East, when my house fell on her and killed her," she replied.

Oz asked, "What do you wish me to do?"

"Send me back to Kansas, where my Aunt Em and Uncle Henry are," she answered earnestly. "I am sure Aunt Em will be dreadfully worried over my being away so long."

"Well," said the Head, "You must do something for me in return. You must kill the Wicked Witch of the West."

"But I cannot!" exclaimed Dorothy, greatly surprised.

"You killed the Witch of the East and you wear the Silver Shoes, which bear a powerful charm. There is now but one Wicked Witch left in all this land, and when you can tell me she is dead I will send you back to Kansas—but not before."

Sorrowfully Dorothy left the throne room and went back to where her friends were waiting to hear what Oz had said to her. "There is no hope for me," she said sadly, "for Oz will not send me home until I have killed the Wicked Witch of the West; and that I can never do."

Her friends were sorry, but could do nothing to help her; so Dorothy went to her room and cried herself to sleep.

The next day, the Scarecrow was called to see Oz. Oz appeared to him as a lovely lady with silky wings.

The following day, the Tin Woodman went to see Oz. Oz appeared as a great monster to him. When the Lion went to see Oz, he was a great ball of fire. Each one of the travelers was asked to kill the Wicked Witch of the West. "What shall we do now?" asked Dorothy sadly.

"There is only one thing we can do," returned the Lion, "and that is to go to the land of the Winkies, seek out the Wicked Witch, and destroy her."

Therefore, it was decided to start upon their journey the next morning.

The soldier with the green whiskers led them through the streets of the Emerald City until they reached the room where the Guardian of the Gates lived. This officer unlocked their spectacles to put them back in his great box, and then he politely opened the gate.

"Which road leads to the Wicked Witch of the West?" asked Dorothy.

"There is no road," answered the Guardian of the Gates. "No one ever wishes to go that way."

"How, then, are we to find her?" inquired the girl.

"That will be easy," replied the man, "for when she knows you are in the country of the Winkies, she will find you, and make you all her slaves. Take care; for she is wicked and fierce, and may not allow you to destroy her. Keep to the West, where the sun sets, and you cannot fail to find her."

The Emerald City was soon left far behind. As they advanced, the ground became hillier and untilled.

In the afternoon the sun shone hot in their faces, for there were no trees to offer them shade; so that before night Dorothy and Toto and the Lion were tired, and lay down upon the grass and fell asleep, with the Woodman and the Scarecrow keeping watch.

The Wicked Witch of the West saw Dorothy and her friends a long distance off from her castle. She was so angry to find them in her country that she blew upon a silver whistle that hung around her neck.

At once there came running to her a great pack of wolves. They had long legs and fierce eyes and sharp teeth.

"Go to those people," said the Witch, "and tear them to pieces."

"Very well," said the wolf leader, and he dashed away at full speed, followed by the others.

It was lucky that the Scarecrow and the Woodman were wide awake and heard the wolves coming.

The Woodman seized his axe and chopped each wolf's head from its body as it came at him. When the Wicked Witch saw all her wolves lying dead, and the strangers still traveling through her country, she became angrier than before. She blew her silver whistle twice.

A great flock of crows came flying toward her. The Wicked Witch said to the King Crow, "Fly at once to the strangers; peck out their eyes and tear them to pieces."

my land and destroy them all, except the Lion," said the Wicked Witch. "Bring him to me, for I will harness him like a horse, and make him work."

The Winged Monkeys flew away to the place where Dorothy and her friends were walking. Some of the Monkeys seized the Tin Woodman and carried him over a country thickly covered with sharp rocks. They dropped the poor Woodman, who fell a great distance to the rocks, where he lay battered and dented.

Other Monkeys caught the Scarecrow and pulled all of the straw out of his clothes and head. The remaining Monkeys tied up the Lion with rope, then lifted him up and flew away with him to the Witch's castle, where he was placed in a small yard with a high iron fence around it, so that he could not escape.

But Dorothy they dared not harm, for the mark of the Good Witch's kiss was upon her forehead. The Winged Monkeys carried Dorothy to the castle, where they set her down upon the front doorstep. Then the leader of the Monkeys said to the Witch:

"We have obeyed you as far as we were able. The Tin Woodman and the Scarecrow are destroyed, and the Lion is tied up in your yard. The little girl we dare not harm, nor the dog she carries in her arms."

Then all the Winged Monkeys, with much chattering and noise, flew out of sight.

The Wicked Witch was both surprised and worried when she saw the mark on Dorothy's forehead and her charmed Silver Shoes, for she dared not hurt the girl in any way. But the Witch saw that

Dorothy did not know the power the Silver Shoes gave her. She thought, "I can still make her my slave, for she does not know how to use her power."

Then the Witch said to Dorothy, harshly and severely:

"Come with me; and see that you mind everything I tell you, for if you do not I will make an end of you, as I did of the Tin Woodman and the Scarecrow."

The Witch put her to work in the kitchen. Dorothy made up her mind to work as hard as she could, for she was glad the Wicked Witch had decided not to kill her. The Lion was kept in the courtyard and not fed until he would obey.

Every night, while the Witch was asleep, Dorothy carried the Lion food from the cupboard. After he had eaten, he would lie down on his bed of straw, and Dorothy would lie beside him and put her head on his soft, shaggy mane, while they talked of their troubles and tried to plan some way to escape. But they could find no way to get out of the castle, for it was constantly guarded by the Winkies, who were the slaves of the Wicked Witch and too afraid of her not to do as she told them.

The Wicked Witch longed to have the Silver Shoes, which the girl always wore, for they were very powerful. To get the Silver Shoes, the Wicked Witch played a trick on Dorothy. She placed a bar of iron in the middle of the kitchen floor, and then using magic, made the iron invisible to human eyes. When Dorothy walked across the floor she stumbled over the bar, not being able to see it, and fell down. She was not much hurt, but in her fall one of the Silver Shoes came off, and before she could reach it, the Witch had snatched it away and put it on her own foot.

Dorothy, seeing that she had lost one of her pretty shoes, grew angry. She picked up a bucket of water and dashed it over the Witch.

Instantly the Wicked Witch gave a loud cry of fear, and then, as Dorothy looked at her in wonder, the Witch melted away.

Dorothy picked out the Silver Shoe, which was all that was left of the old woman, cleaned and dried it with a cloth, and put it on her foot again. Then she ran out to the courtyard, where she set the Lion free and told him that the Wicked Witch of the West was dead. They went into the castle, where Dorothy called all the Winkies together and told them that they were no longer slaves.

There was great rejoicing among the yellow Winkies, for they had been made to work hard for many years for the Wicked Witch.

The Winkies thanked Dorothy by finding and fixing the Tin Woodman and the Scarecrow, who had been hurt by the Winged Monkeys. There was much rejoicing as all the travelers were reunited.

The next day the travelers bade the Winkies good-bye, for they were going back to the Emerald City to have Oz grant their wishes. The Winkies had grown so fond of the Tin Woodman that they begged him to come back and rule over them and the Yellow Land of the West.

Using the Witch's Golden Cap, Dorothy called the Winged Monkeys to carry them to Oz. In the Emerald City, they were admitted

at once to see Oz. Each one of them expected to see the Wizard in the shape he had taken before, and all were greatly surprised when they saw no one in the room. The room was very still.

Presently they heard a solemn Voice, that seemed to come from somewhere near the top of the great dome, say:

"I am Oz, the Great and Terrible. Why do you seek me?"

"We have come to claim our promise, O Oz. Dorothy has killed the Wicked Witch," said the Tin Woodman.

"Is the Wicked Witch really destroyed?" asked the Voice.

"Yes," Dorothy answered, "I melted her with a bucket of water."

"Well, come to me tomorrow," said Oz.

"We shan't wait a day longer," replied the Scarecrow.

"You must keep your promises to us!" exclaimed Dorothy.

The Lion gave a loud roar, which made Toto jump away from him in alarm and tip over the screen that stood in a corner. Standing where the screen had been was a little old man, with a bald head and a wrinkled face, who seemed to be as much surprised as they were. The Tin Woodman asked, "Who are you?"

"I am Oz, the Great and Terrible," said the little man, in a trembling voice. "Please don't hurt me."

"I thought Oz was a great Head," said Dorothy.

"And I thought Oz was a lovely Lady," said the Scarecrow.

"And I thought Oz was a terrible Beast," said the Tin Woodman.

"And I thought Oz was a Ball of Fire," exclaimed the Lion.

"Are you not a Great Wizard?"

"No, I have been making believe. I am just a common man. Please don't tell or I shall be punished," he said.

"What about my brains?" asked the Scarecrow.

"Or my heart?" asked the Woodman.

"Or my courage?" asked the Lion.

"How shall I ever get home?" asked Dorothy.

"If you come back tomorrow, I shall help you all," said Oz. "I have played the Wizard so long that one more day won't matter."

The next morning the Scarecrow went to see Oz. Oz filled the Scarecrow's head with pins and needles, to make him "sharp". He cut a hole in the Woodman's chest and placed in it a small silk heart. To the Lion he gave a potion he called "courage." Then he turned to Dorothy.

"In order to get home," he said, "you must sew a big balloon out of silk. We will fill it with hot air to make it rise. It will carry us home over the desert."

"Us?" asked Dorothy. "Are you going with me?"

"Yes," said Oz. "I am from Omaha myself. I came here in a balloon a long time ago."

"I shall be glad to have your company," said Dorothy.

"Thank you," he answered. "Now, if you will help me sew the silk together, we will make our balloon."

When the balloon was made, Oz sent word to his people that he was going to visit a great brother Wizard who lived in the clouds. The news spread rapidly throughout the city and everyone came to see the wonderful sight.

Oz got into the balloon's basket and said to the people:

"I am now going away to make a visit. While I am gone the Scarecrow will rule over you. I command you to obey him as you would me."

The balloon was tugging hard at the rope that held it to the ground, for the air within it was hot, making the balloon rise.

"Come, Dorothy!" cried the Wizard. "Hurry up, or the balloon will fly away."

"I can't find Toto anywhere," replied Dorothy. Toto had run into the crowd to bark at a kitten, and Dorothy at last found him. She picked him up and ran towards the balloon.

She was within a few steps of it, and Oz was holding out his hands to help her into the basket, when, crack! went the ropes, and the balloon rose into the air without her.

"Come back!" she screamed. "I want to go, too!"

"I can't come back, my dear," called Oz from the basket. "Good-bye!"

"Good-bye!" everyone shouted.

Dorothy wept bitterly at the passing of her hope to get home to Kansas again; but when she thought it all over she was glad she had not gone up in a balloon. She also felt sorry at losing Oz, and so did her companions.

The Scarecrow was now the ruler of the Emerald City. The morning after the balloon had gone up with Oz, the four travelers met in the throne room and talked matters over.

The Scarecrow sat in the big throne and the others stood respect-fully before him.

The Scarecrow was thinking, and his head bulged out so horribly that Dorothy feared it would burst.

"Let us call in the soldier with the green whiskers," he said, "and ask his advice on how to get Dorothy home."

So the soldier was summoned and entered the throne room.

"Is there anyone who can help me get home?" asked Dorothy.

"Glinda, the Good Witch of the South, might. She is the most powerful of all the Witches."

"How can I get to her castle?" asked Dorothy.

"The road is to the South," he answered, "but it is full of danger."

The soldier then left them and the Scarecrow said:

"It seems that the best thing Dorothy can do is to travel to the Land of the South and ask Glinda to help her. If Dorothy stays here she will never get back to Kansas."

They all agreed to start out for Glinda's castle the next morning.

The first day's journey was through the green fields and bright flowers that surrounded the Emerald City. Soon they came to a thick wood. The Scarecrow tried to walk under a tree with wide-spreading branches, but was flung back. This did not hurt the Scarecrow, but it surprised him. He walked up to another tree, but its branches immedi-ately seized him and tossed him back again.

The Woodman walked up to a tree and, when it tried to seize him, he cut it in two.

"Come on!" he shouted to the others. "Be quick!" They all ran forward and passed under the tree. The other trees of the forest did nothing to keep them back.

At the far edge of the wood they reached a wall made of china, which they made a ladder for and climbed over.

Before them was a great stretch of country with a floor as smooth and shining and white as the bottom of a big platter. Scattered around were many small houses and barns made of china, painted in the brightest colors. There were cows and sheep and horses and pigs and chickens, all made of china.

The people were milkmaids, shepherdesses, shepherds, princesses, and princes all made of china, even their clothes. They were so small that the tallest of them was no higher than Dorothy's knee. A jolly little clown with many cracks walked toward them, and Dorothy could see that in spite of his pretty clothes of red and yellow and green he had been mended in many places. The china people broke easily, so the travelers walked carefully through the country.

After climbing over another china wall, the travelers soon came to a gloomy forest. The Lion thought it was a wonderful forest, and that he would like to live there.

Before they had gone far they heard a low rumble, as of the growling of many wild animals. They came to an opening in the wood, in which were gathered hundreds of tigers and elephants and bears and wolves and foxes. The Lion explained that the animals were holding a meeting, and he judged by their snarling and growling that they were in great trouble.

As he spoke several of the beasts caught sight of him, and at once the great assemblage hushed as if by magic. The biggest of the tigers came up to the Lion and bowed, saying:

"Welcome, O King of Beasts! You have come in good time to fight our enemy and bring peace to all the animals of the forest once more."

"What is your trouble?" asked the Lion quietly.

"We are all threatened," answered the tiger, "by a tremendous monster, like a great spider, which has lately come into this forest. Not one of us is safe while this fierce creature is alive. We had called a meeting to decide how to take care of ourselves when you came among us."

"Where is this great spider now?" asked the Lion.

"There, among the oak trees," said the tiger.

The lion went to find the great spider. It was lying asleep when the Lion found him. He pounced upon the spider and knocked off his head, which had been placed upon a slender neck.

The Lion went back to where the beasts of the forest were waiting for him and said proudly:

"You need fear your enemy no longer."

Then the beasts bowed down to the Lion as their King, and he promised to come back and rule over them as soon as Dorothy was safely on her way to Kansas.

The four travelers came upon a steep hill, covered with great pieces of rock. They had just started forward when a voice said, "Keep back! This hill belongs to us, and no one may cross it." The man speaking stepped out from behind a rock. He was very short, with a big flat-

topped head and a thick neck full of wrinkles. The man had no arms. The Scarecrow was not afraid of him, and started forward.

As quick as lightning the man's neck shot forward and his flat-topped head struck the Scarecrow, sending him tumbling down the hill. Almost as quickly as it came forward the head went back to the body, and the man laughed harshly as he said, "It isn't as easy as you think!"

Laughter came from the other rocks, and Dorothy saw hundreds of the armless Hammer-Heads upon the hillside, one behind every rock. She saw that there was no way around the Hammer-Heads, so she called the Winged Monkeys to carry the travelers to Glinda's castle.

Standing before the gates of the castle were three girls, dressed in red uniforms trimmed with gold braid. They inquired as to who the travelers were, then with Glinda's permission, led them into the castle.

They followed the soldier girls into a big room where Glinda sat upon a throne of rubies.

She was both beautiful and young to their eyes. Her hair was a rich red in color and fell in flowing ringlets over her shoulders. Her dress was pure white, and her eyes were blue.

"What can I do for you, my child?" she asked kindly.

Dorothy told the Witch of her adventures, and replied:

"My greatest wish now is to get back to Kansas."

"I am sure I can tell you of a way to get back to Kansas," Glinda said. "But first you must give me the Golden Cap."

Dorothy then gave Glinda the Golden Cap, and the Witch asked the Scarecrow, the Tin Woodman, and the Lion: "What will you do when Dorothy has left us?"

"I will return to the Emerald City as its ruler," the Scarecrow replied.

"I will rule the Winkies," said the Tin Woodman.

"And I will rule the forest," said the Lion.

"My first command to the Winged Monkeys," said Glinda, "shall be to carry you all to your homes. Your Silver Shoes will carry you over the desert," Glinda told Dorothy, "Just click them together three times and say where you wish to go."

"I think I should like to go back to Kansas right away," said Dorothy.

Dorothy hugged and kissed her friends and Glinda goodbye, thanking Glinda for all the kindness she had shown to her friends and herself. It was a sad parting.

Dorothy held Toto in her arms, and having said one last good-bye she clapped the heels of her shoes together three times, saying:

"Take me home to Aunt Em!"

Instantly she was whirling through the air so swiftly that all she could see or feel was the wind whistling past her ears.

The Silver Shoes took but three steps, and then stopped so suddenly that Dorothy rolled over upon the grass several times before she knew where she was.

"Good gracious!" Dorothy cried, looking about her.

She was sitting on the broad Kansas prairie, and before her was

the new farmhouse Uncle Henry built after the cyclone had carried away the old one. Uncle Henry was milking the cows in the barnyard, and Toto had jumped out of her arms and was running toward the barn, barking furiously.

Dorothy stood up and found she was in her stocking-feet. The Silver Shoes had fallen off in her flight through the air, and were lost forever in the desert.

Aunt Em had just come out of the house when she saw Dorothy running toward her.

"My darling child!" she cried, hugging Dorothy and covering her face with kisses. "Where in the world did you come from?"

"From the Land of Oz," said Dorothy. "And here is Toto, too. And oh, Aunt Em! I'm so glad to be at home again!"